NEW LONGMAN LITERATURE

Nightjohn

Gary Paulsen

PEARSON

Longman

Edinburgh Gate
Harlow, Essex

Pearson Education Limited
Edinburgh Gate
Harlow
Essex
CM20 2JE
England

First published in Great Britain in 1994 by Macmillan Children's
Books, London

This educational edition first published by Pearson Education 2006

ISBN-10: 1-4058-2063-2
ISBN-13: 978-1-4058-2063-9

Printed in China
EPC/01

The Publisher's policy is to use paper manufactured from sustainable
forests.

Contents

This book is dedicated to the memory of Sally Hemmings, who was owned, raised and subsequently used by Thomas Jefferson without benefit of ever drawing a single free breath.

Except for variations in time and character identification and placement, the events written in this story are true and actually happened.

One

This is a story about Nightjohn. I guess in some ways it is a story about me just as much because I am in it and I know what happened and some of it happened to me but it still seems to be most about him.

Nightjohn.

There's some to say I brought him with witchin', brought Nightjohn because he came to be talking to me alone but it ain't so. I knew he was coming but it wasn't witchin', just listening.

It happened. How it came to be was that Nightjohn he came and it wasn't me, wasn't nobody one or the other brought him except maybe it was that God did it, made Nightjohn to come.

God and maybe old Clel Waller. He wants that we should call him 'master', and they's some do when he can hear but we call him dog droppings and pig slop and worse things yet when he ain't listening nor close. He ain't no master of nobody except that he's got dogs and a whip and a gun and so can cause hurt to be on some, bad hurt, but he ain't no master for all of that. We just call him that when we have to. Keeps him from whipping on us.

I'm Sarny and they be thinking I'm dumb and maybe up to witchin' and got a stuck tongue because when I birthed they say I come out wrong, come out all backwards and twixt-and-twist. But it ain't so that I'm dumb. I'm just quiet and they be thinking because I don't make noise and go to twattering all the time that I be dumb. But I ain't. I just be so quiet and listen all the time that I learn things.

I'm Sarny and the other part of my name be the same as old Waller who wants to be master but is nothing. Nothing. I don't count the back part of my name no more than I count old Waller himself. No more than I count spit.

My mammy she told me that my birthing mammy was sold when I was four years old because she was a good breeder and Waller he needed the money. My mammy said that my birthing mammy brought enough for four field hands and that she cried when the man bought her. My mammy say that my birthing mammy stood in the back of a wagon and watched back and waved and my mammy held me up so I could see the waving and hear her crying. But I don't remember that.

All I know for a mammy is the one that raised me, old Delie, and she be the one who raises all the young. Breeders don't get to keep their own babies because they be spending all their time raising babies and not working. So when they're born babies go to the wet nurse and she feeds them and then old Delie gets them and they don't live with their birthing mammies again even if they aren't sold off.

It isn't for certain how old I am except for the sticks. Mammy keeps a stick for each one of us and in the summer she cuts a notch on the stick for each of the girls so as to know when it will come time for the troubles and then the breeding. Waller puts great store in the sticks and watches them like a old hawk watching the chicken pens.

By the stick I am going into the same year as all the fingers on both hands, fold them down, then hold up the thumbs. Delie says it be twelve but I don't know numbers to count so that doesn't mean so much to me. I don't yet have the trouble so I am still left to be as a child. We work around the quarters and clean the yard and gather eggs and help mammy with the young ones. It's work, but it ain't dawn to dark hard work like the field work and it leaves me a bit of time to listen and see things. Mammy she tells me some things to learn and I hear some others from the field hands who come back at dark and now and again I have to work in the flower beds below the big window on the white house.

The house women are fond of leaving the window open and talking all their business right there. So when I'm in the flower bed below the window I hear more things to learn. When the day is coming on dark and we are all finished eating out of the trough in the front of the quarters I get onto the pallet in the back of the long log house with Delie and the babies and I lays there and thinks.

I thinks of all the things I have learned that day and then I tries to add them to the things I learned the day before and then the day before that. I've been doing that as long as I can remember, since I was almost just walking, and I remember all the parts of my life. If there is time of an evening and I haven't been worked to the bone I can just lay there in the dark and think on all my time and remember it. Except for my birthing mammy – I can't think on her at all except to wonder and wonder about her.

Did she have dark skin or light? How was her voice, how did it sound? But you can't remember what isn't there and no amount of thinking on it will make it come into my brain.

It was in the flower bed that I first heard about Nightjohn. Not by name, but by happening.

Two

One morning I was below the window working in the roses. Some leaves had fallen because of the little green bugs that eat the roses and I had to chew tobacco leaves and spit on the plants to kill the bugs. I didn't much like to chew on tobacco leaves, though some of the men favoured it, and it made me sick enough to near heave my guts. I had to stop and while I was stopped, just under the window down in the thick leaves and the soft dirt, I hears it.

'I swear – if Clel doesn't stop buying hands we won't have any money left for dresses.' It was the missus talking to her sister. Her sister be an older woman never found a man, dried up and mean and she hates us. The missus is named Margaret and her sister named Alaine or something close to that. Course we never call them by their names. Never talk to them at all. And when we talk about them in the quarters and ain't nobody listening but quarters' people we call them same as the master. Call them dog droppings or horse crap.

'He went out and bought another hand,' the missus said. 'Over a thousand dollars. Honestly, he must think we're made of money.'

I didn't know counting but I knew a little of money. Once I found a penny in the dirt by the quarters and I went to mammy and held it out.

'Hide that,' she told me. 'That's money. Somebody see that and they'll come along and take it from you.'

So I figured money was something to have and keep and I kept the penny, hid in the dirt at the end of the quarters and I still have it. Sometimes I take it out when there ain't anybody around and rub it on my shirtdress until it shines and shines.

And I knew that there was bigger money than a penny but I didn't know how that all worked, that bigger money, because it wasn't something I learned. So when the missus she said about a new hand costing a thousand dollars all I knew was that it was more than a penny. More than many pennies. Maybe more than all the pennies in the world because they be rich, the people in the white house.

Richer than God, mammy said once, but she was just mad and didn't mean it. She'd been praying and got caught at it. People in the quarters weren't supposed to pray nor know nothing about God. Mammy she prayed all the time, in her head. Usually she only prayed out loud late at night when there wasn't anybody to hear her. Sometimes she brought in the big cast iron kettle used for making morning food to pour in the trough for us to eat.

Mammy would put the kettle in the corner of the quarters, way back in the dark corner, and put her head inside the kettle so's the sound wouldn't carry and she'd pray in a whisper. She swore they could hear like cats up to the big house and the only way to keep safe was to pray in the kettle.

I one time put my head in the kettle with her.

'Lord Jesus,' she said, talking to the bottom of the kettle. 'Lord Jesus, you come be making us free. Free someday. In your name, amen.'

I was small then and didn't know about being free, or even how to think about being free, or even what being free meant. So I asked her what free meant.

'Nothing to talk about now,' she said. 'You'll know when you get older but now you just be quiet and never, never say you heard me praying about being free.'

Which I never did, even after I learned what freedom is and started praying for it my ownself. Even then.

The people in the white house aren't richer than God, I know that.

But they be rich, and they be spending a lot of money and they brought in the new hand for a thousand dollars.

And that be Nightjohn.

Three

Old Waller brought him in bad.

Sometimes they come in not so bad. Spec'lators bring them to sell sometimes all in a wagon, sell them from the wagon and Waller he buys them one or two or whatever, right from the wagon.

Sometimes Waller he goes for to buy them at some other place and brings them home in the wagon, sitting in the back. Old Waller on the seat with a pistol in his belt, sitting like he thinks he's big. Other places, near here, other places have what they call overseers to use the whip and to use the gun and go to get them. But not here. Waller he loves to carry the whip and carry the gun and so he rides in the wagon his ownself and makes on to be big. Sitting there like he don't know we hate him.

But he can bring them in good or he can bring them in bad and with Nightjohn he brought him in bad.

Not in the wagon. He was walking, all alone in front of the horse. Waller riding the big brown horse in back. Had a rope down and over to a shackle on Nightjohn's neck. Rope tied to the saddle. So when the horse stopped, Nightjohn he stopped, jerked on his neck.

Waller he brought Nightjohn into the main yard near the quarters out in the open, yelling and swearing at him. Yanking on the rope. Nightjohn he didn't have any clothes on, stood naked in the sun. I was by the quarters, carrying water to wash the eating trough before it was time for the evening feeding and I saw them.

Standing in the sun with the rope going from his neck up to the saddle, tired and sweating because Waller ran him. Dust all over him. Flies around his shoulders.

His back was all over scars from old whippings. The skin across his shoulders and down was raised in ripples, thick as my hand, up and down his back and onto his rear end and down his legs some.

I wondered why he was bought with all the marks. When they be marked that way people don't buy them because it means they hard to work, hard to get to work.

But he did. Waller he brought Nightjohn home and ran him naked till he sweated and the biting flies took at him and I was there and saw him come in.

I'm brown. Same as dark sassafras tea. But I had seen black people, true black. And Nightjohn was that way. Beautiful. So black he was like the marble stone by the front of the white house; so black it seemed I could see inside, down into him. See almost through him somehow.

In a little, Waller he untied the rope. Then he cracked the whip once or twice like he be a big man and drives Nightjohn past the quarters and out to the field to work. Didn't matter that he'd been run or might be thirsty. He didn't stop at the pump but ran him right on through and out to the fields, naked as he was born, to get to hoeing.

He come in bad and it wasn't until late that night, after dark in the quarters, that I learned his name.

Mammy she made canvas pants for the new men when they came. Sewed them from the roll of tarp-cloth we used for all our clothes. She gave a pair to Nightjohn when they came in from the field but he didn't have time to say nothing because it was time for the evening food.

Two times a day at the wooden trough – that's how we eat. Mornings they pour buttermilk down the trough and we dip cornbread in it and sometimes pieces of pork fat. We take turns on a calabash gourd for a dipper to get all the milk out except the little ones don't always get much of a turn and have to lick the bottom of the trough when it's done. For midday meal the field hands – men and women both, 'less a woman is a breeder in her last month, then she can work the yard – each carry a piece of cornbread and pork fat or meat with them. When the sun is high overhead they stop long enough to stand and eat the bread and fat. They don't get to sit or rest. Even do they have to do their business they dig a hole with their hoe and do it standing and cover it with dirt and get back to work.

Don't they do this, don't they do it right, don't they keep standing and work even to eat and do their business, don't they do it all just exactly right the whip comes down on them. Old Waller he don't have overseers but they's two men he calls drivers. They have whips and clubs and use them.

Then at night, when it's just dark they come in from the fields. During the day mammy and the breeders that can still walk and the small ones that can't keep up to work in the fields yet make food.

We cook in the big pot mammy used for praying. We cook pork fat and vegetables from the garden and make skillet cornbread. When the field people come in at night we pour from the pot in the trough and everybody passes the gourd and eats with their hands and dips cornbread into the juice till it's gone. Then the young ones get to lick the trough and we go into the quarters for the night.

There ain't no light allowed in the quarters. Time was, mammy said, when she had a small bowl and made a lamp with a piece of cotton and melted pork fat but up to the white house they saw the light and made her put it out. Kept the workers awake, they said.

Course we be awake anyway, if we want to. Just be awake in the dark. Light comes through the open door and there are four small windows down the back wall. If there's a moon there be good light, light enough to see faces and talk and even if there isn't a moon enough comes from the stars and the lights from the white house to let us see a little.

Those to work in the field are always tired. Always caved in with work. And there ain't never enough to eat, so they be hungry, too. They usually go to sleep as soon as they hit the corn-shuck pallets on the floor.

But the first night when the new man was there you could tell it was going to be different. He didn't even get on the floor but went right over to the corner where mammy put the pot to pray sometimes and sat there. The new canvas pants were so stiff I could hear them crackle and bend when he sat back against the wall. I was on the side of mammy's shuck mattress along with about half a dozen young ones who were all kicking and scratching so sleep wasn't coming and I hear:

'Who's got tobacco? I need some tobacco.'

11

It was a whisper, but loud, cutting from the corner where the new man sat. I had me some tobacco. It was just shredded bottom leaf that I'd been chewing to spit on the roses but I'd kept some back in a wrapped piece of sacking inside my shirtdress, tied round my waist on a piece of string. I didn't say a word. You come on things, things to keep, and you keep them to trade for other things. Things you need. Like pork fat. Or pennies.

He chuckled, low and rippling. Sounded like a low wind through willows, that small laugh, or maybe water moving over round rocks. Deep and soft.

'I'll trade,' he whispered. 'I'll trade something for a lip of tobacco.'

I thought, What you got to trade? You come in naked as the day you was born, come in bad with whip marks all up and down your back, not even a set of clothes or canvas pants and you're ready to go to trading? I didn't say it, but I thought it. And he like to read my thoughts.

'What I got to trade, what I got to trade for a lip of tobacco is letters. I knows letters. I'll trade A, B, and C for a lip of chew.' He laughed again.

And there I was, with the tobacco in my dress and he said that and I didn't know what letters was, nor what they meant, but I thought it might be something I wanted to know. To learn.

So mammy she was sleeping, her breath moving in and out, and I wiggled out of the pile of young ones and moved to the dark corner and set my ownself next to him. 'What's a letter?'

He smiled. 'You sound like you've got tobacco.'

12

'Not until I know what a letter is....'

'Why, it's reading. You learn the letters first and then when you know them you string them together into words. I'll trade you three letters for a lipful.'

I knew about reading. It was something that the people in the white house did from paper. They could read words on paper. But we weren't allowed to be reading. We weren't allowed to understand or read nothing but once I saw some funny lines on the side of a feed sack. It said:

100 lbs

I wrote them down in the dirt with a stick and mammy gave me a smack on the back of the head that like to drove me into the ground.

'Don't you take to that, take to writing,' she said.

'I wasn't doing it. I was just copying something I saw on a feed sack.'

'Don't. They catch you doing that and they'll think you're learning to read. You learn to read and they'll whip you till your skin hangs like torn rags. Or cut your thumb off. Stay away from writing and reading.'

So I did. But I remembered how it had looked, the drawings on the sack and in the dirt, and it still puzzled me. I dug in my dress and found the tobacco but held it.

'You saying you can read?' He nodded.

'I give you something to read, you can read it? Just like that?'

'I can.'

There was some yellow light from the windows of the big house and it came through the doorway and made a light patch on the dirt floor.

'Come on.'

I led him to the light patch and squatted. I used my finger to scratch what I remembered in the dirt. The floor was hard packed and I had to rub hard to make it show right.

'There.'

He squatted and squinted.

'Why, those ain't letters. Those are numbers.'

'Numbers?'

He nodded. 'Sure is. Says one hundred. Then there's those three letters on the end. They don't work for me as a word. Just L B S – don't say a word. It must mean something to somebody.'

'Can you teach me that?'

'To read?'

'To read what I just put there in the dirt – can you teach me?'

He rubbed his chin. 'Well, mought be if I had some tobacco....'

I dug the sack out of my shirtdress and gave him a pinch. He put it in the side of his mouth.

'Way it works,' he said, 'is you got to learn all the letters and numbers before you can learn to read. You got to learn the alphabet.'

'Alphabet?'

He nodded. 'There be lots of letters, and each one means something different. You got to learn each one.'

'Those three you said back in the dark corner? Can you teach me those?'

'I sure can.' He used the edge of his hand to rub out

14

what I had written in the dirt. Then he made a drawing with his thumb.

A

'Tonight we just do *A*.' He sat back on his heels and pointed. 'There it be.'

I looked at it, wondered how it stood. 'Where's the bottom to it?'

'There. It stands on two feet, just like you.'

'What does it mean?'

'It means *A* – just like I said. It's the first letter in the alphabet. And when you see it you make a sound like this: *ayyy*, or *ahhhh*.'

'That's reading? To make that sound?'

He nodded. 'When you see that letter on paper or a sack or in the dirt you make one of those sounds. That's reading.'

'Well that ain't hard at all.'

He laughed. That same low roll. Made me think of thunder long ways off, moving in a summer sky. 'There's more to it. Other letters. But that's it.'

'Why they be cutting our thumbs off if we learn to read – if that's all it is?'

''Cause to know things, for us to know things, is bad for them. We get to wanting and when we get to wanting it's bad for them. They thinks we want what they got.'

I thought of what they had. Fine clothes and food. I heard one of the house workers say they ate off plates and had forks and spoons and knives and wiped their mouths like they wiped their butts. 'That's true – I want it.'

'That's why they don't want us reading.' He sighed. 'I

15

got to rest now. They run me ten miles in a day and worked me into the ground. I need some sleep.'

He moved back to the corner and settled down and I curled up to mammy in amongst the young ones again.

A, I thought. *Ayyy, ahhhh*. There it is. I be reading.

'Hey there in the corner,' I whispered.

'What?'

'What's your name?'

'I be John.'

'I be Sarny.'

'Go to sleep, Sarny.'

But I didn't. I snuggled into mammy and pulled a couple of the young ones in for heat and kept my eyes open so I wouldn't sleep and thought:

A

Four

Come a hard time then.

Come a awful, hard time.

There be a girl before then named Alice. She slept in the other end of the quarters and as soon as she got big she went to work in the fields picking and hoeing. But she was addled in the head, off dreaming sometimes, and mammy said one day that they would sell her. But her body was all right and they in the white house decided she be a good breeder so they set her for that.

She didn't take well to it and fought and they tied her to make it happen, in the breeding shed back of the quarters but it went bad on her head and her thinking. When it was done she was worse than before.

She wandered in the yard and sometimes even went up to the white house. Except for the house servants and gardening we weren't allowed to the white house and when the master one day caught Alice he took her to the wall of the spring house.

The spring house was where we got drinking water. If was made of stone and with heavy walls. They had rings of iron to be made in the walls many years past, big rings of iron with chains and shackles and they put Alice there and tore her clothes off.

Then the master he whipped her his ownself with a rawhide whip cut from an old gin belt used on the cotton gin. Sometimes he doesn't whip and makes a field hand do it and stands with his pistol in his belt and smiles.

But sometimes he likes to take the whip and this time he

whipped her until her back was all ripped and bleeding. We had to watch. Every time there was somebody to be on the wall of the spring house and be whipped or other punishments we all had to watch.

When it was done and she had screamed until she sounded like pigs being cut he made mammy to go to the salt house and get salt and rub it in the cuts to make more pain.

I never heard a sound like that. I'd seen men whipped but never that kind of sound, cutting like that, high and higher until it whistled in my ears.

Then he left her to hang there until the next day. The flies they came and mammy went out and covered her back with a cloth and kept some of them off so they wouldn't make maggots in the cuts.

Next morning they took her down and they was some maggot eggs but not so bad. I helped mammy clean Alice. We took her in the quarters and mammy she rubbed grease on Alice's back and I sat and held her hands because she kept trying to reach around and push mammy's hand away.

All the time she don't say anything. Not a thing. Not even the silly things she used to say and when we were done she lay on the floor in the corner like she was broken. Broken inside.

Mammy made her some root tea that smelled of bark but Alice wouldn't drink it. She just lay there all that night and the next three, four days. During that time John came and I talked to him about A, traded tobacco with him. For two nights he didn't do no work on the trade and went to sleep right after the trough because the master worked him so hard. On the third night after I traded for A – sometime that same night Alice ran.

My life is short, but some live long and the one thing we know, short or long – it's wrong to run. Not wrong because it's wrong. But wrong because nobody ever gets away.

I've seen two to try it. Both men. One was an old man named Jim who just couldn't take no more and one night he up and cut.

They set after him the next morning with dogs. Only the master, he don't only go his ownself but took five or six field hands with him to see so they can carry what they see back to tell us.

The dogs be mean. He feeds them things to make them mean. Blood things. Sometimes he'll take them to the fields, and should a man or woman work a little behind the others, or behind the best man, who is whipped to speed – why, he sets the dog on the slow one. And he don't pull them off right away, neither. Lets them go until they taste blood and want more of it.

They's mean, the dogs. They's big and red with tight hair and heads like hogs and mean as Waller his ownself. He keep them in a stone pen by the side of the horse barn and they slobber and chew at the gate each time we walk by. Dirt mean.

Jim, he ran at night too but it didn't help. The field hands told us later. He cut and ran down to the river, ran in the water for a goodly distance then on the top of a fence rail for as long as the fence ran and then dropped to the ground and just moved.

The dogs followed him all the way. The hands said that one dog even got up and ran on the top rail of the fence. Only took half a day and they caught Jim.

The last bit, when he heard the dogs singing him, baying on him, Jim climbed a tree. Problem was, the tree wasn't higher than he could reach, nearly, and as high as he got, the bottom of him hung down where the dogs could reach him.

The master set the dogs on him and they tore and ripped what they could reach until there wasn't any meat on Jim's legs or bottom. The dogs ripped it all off, to hang in shreds. The field hands say he still didn't let go, nor never did. Even when he was dead his hands didn't let go and the master made the field hands leave him there. They's some wanted to take Jim down and bury him but he made them to leave him that way, hanging by his hands in the tree, for the birds to eat.

Second man was young. Name of Pawley. He wasn't a big enough hand to be allowed to be a breeder in the quarters and so he went to looking. He snucked away and met a girl at a plantation down the road a piece and they sat in the moonlight with each other some nights. Pawley he made it back before wake-up time every night but one, the last one. He fell asleep in his girl's arms, fell asleep in the moonlight.

So they from the white house set out with the dogs and Pawley he didn't run, or try to get away. He was on his way home but they let the dogs to have him anyway, tear him up to bleed but not kill him. Then the master he tied him down and cut him like he did the cattle so he wouldn't run to girls no more, but the cut went wrong and Cawley he laid all night and bled to death without ever making a sound in the corner of the quarters.

So don't nobody run. Besides, I don't think there's a place to run to. I heard talk once of some land, some land north but it's far away and it was only talk. Not something to know. Just something to hear. Like birds singing, the talk of the land north, or the wind in the trees. But Alice cut and run that night.

She didn't get far. Down to the river and then sideways some. Her back was still ripped and sore and she must have moved slow. She might have kept moving all night but hadn't gone more than to the other end of the cotton fields – an easy small walk. Then she pulled herself under some brambles and was there when they found her.

He let the dogs to have her.

Didn't matter what she'd gone through, or that her thinking wasn't working right. The field hands with him told us he smiled his big white smile like the big white house, pale maggot white like his skin smile and let the dogs to have her. She didn't fight them or try to get away and they just tore at her. Tore at her until her whole front was torn and gone and she was bleeding from the chest.

She didn't die.

Alice be too tough for her ownself good. She didn't die and he made the hands to carry her back and put her in the quarters. Mammy sewed up what she could with canvas thread and greased and patched and she lived.

She be like Pawley. She didn't make sounds even while mammy was pulling at the torn flaps of skin and sewing

21

them on her chest. Not a sound. Just stared and stared at the wall.

That night John called to me as he came past where I was trying to sleep.

'Tobacco girl – time for another letter.'

I had been all day helping mammy and was tired and sad for Alice, how she be at the other end of the quarters, but I went just the same. I still had two letters coming for that first pinch of tobacco.

He was sitting on his heels in the open doorway.

I squatted next to him. 'What's the next one?'

He used a stick with a sharpened end on it and wiggled in the dirt two half circles:

B

'*Bee*,' he said. 'It be *B*.'

'That sounds crazy.'

'That's how you say the letter. *B*. It's for *behh* or *be* or *buh* or *boo*. That's how a *B* looks and how you make the sound.'

I made it sound in my mouth, whispering. 'So where's the bottom to it?'

'I swear – you always want to know the bottom to things. Here, here it is. It sits on itself this way, facing so the two round places push to the front.'

Suddenly he's gone. One second he's there, the next he's slammed sideways and gone.

'What in the *hell* are you doing to her?'

Mammy was standing there, big and black and tall in the moonlight. 'What you doing to this girl?'

She had come from the side and fetched John such a blow on his head that it knocked him back into the wall and on his back.

He come up quick and didn't cower none.

'Nothing. Not like you think. I'm teaching her to read.'

'That's what I mean,' mammy said. 'What in the *hell* are you doing? Don't you know what they do to her if they find her trying to read? We already got one girl tore to pieces by the whip and the dogs. We don't need two.'

I'd been quiet all this time, watching. Didn't seem so bad, what he was doing. Teaching me a few letters to know. Maybe a word or two. So I said it. 'Doesn't seem so bad – '

'*Bad*?' Then she hissed like a snake. 'Child, they'll cut your thumbs off if you learn to read. They'll whip you until your back looks knitted – until it looks like his back.' She pointed to John, big old finger. 'Is that how you got whipped?'

He shook his head. 'I ran.'

'And got caught.'

'Not the first time.'

She waited. I waited.

'First time I ran I got clean away. I went north, all the way. I was free.'

I'd never heard such a thing. We couldn't even talk about being free. And here was a man said he had been free by running north. I thought, How can that be?

'You ran and got away?' mammy asked.

'I did.'

'You ran until you were clean away?'

'I did.'

'And you came *back*?'

'I did.'

'Why?'

He sighed and it sounded like his voice, like his laugh. Low and way off thunder. It made me think he was going to promise something, the way thunder promises rain. 'For this.'

'What you mean – this?'

'To teach reading.'

It's never quiet in the quarters. During the day the young ones run and scrabble and fight or cry and they's always a gaggle of them. At night everybody be sleeping. But not quiet. Alice, she's quiet. But they's some of them to cry. New workers who are just old enough to be working in the fields cry sometimes in their sleep. They hurt and their hands bleed and pain them from new blisters that break and break again. Old workers cry because they're old and getting to the end and have old pain. Same pain, young and old. Some snore. Others just breathe loud.

It's a long building and dark except for the light coming in the door and the small windows, but it's never quiet. Not even at night.

Now it seemed quiet. Mammy she looked down at John. Didn't say nothing for a long time. Just looked.

I had to think to hear the breathing, night sounds.

Finally mammy talks. Her voice is soft. 'You came back to teach reading?'

John nodded. 'That's half of it.'

'What's the other half?'

'Writing.' He smiled. 'Course, I wasn't going to get caught. I had in mind moving, moving around. Teaching a little here, a little there. Going to do hidey-schools. But I got slow and they got fast and some crackers caught me in the woods. They were hunting bear, but the dogs came on me instead and I took to a tree and they got me.'

Another long quiet. Way off, down by the river, I heard the sound of a nightbird. Singing for day. Soon the sun would come.

'Why does it matter?' Mammy leaned against the wall. She had one hand on the logs, one on her cheek. Tired. 'Why do that to these young ones? To Sarny here. If they learn to read – '

'And write.'

'And write, it's just grief for them. Longtime grief. They find what they don't have, can't have. It ain't good to know that. It eats at you then – to know it and not have it.'

'They have to be able to write,' John said. Voice pushing. He stood and reached out one hand with long fingers and touched mammy on the forehead. It was almost like he be kissing her with his fingers. Soft. Touch like black cotton in the dark. 'They have to read and write. We all have to read and write so we can write about this – what they doing to us. It has to be written.'

Mammy she turned and went back to her mat on the floor. Moving quiet, not looking back. She settled next to the young ones and John he turned to me and he say:

'Next is C.'

Five

Come more hard times.

A week goes by, then another week. It's the time of year for planting and the field hands have to work until they drop. Waller whips them past that and they get so tired they don't know up from down.

But John works with me. Not each night, because he's too tired. Some of them to work in the fields can't even walk back. Have to be carried by others. But some nights he works with me.

I learn a whole family of letters. All the fingers on one hand, two on the other. A, B, C, D, E, F, and G. He makes me to write them in the dirt and shows me how to take more than one of them and make a word, how the word is to be looking and how the word is to be sounding.

'Make it slow, make the sound each time. First the letter, then the sound, then make it to meet the sound from the next letter. Write B, say it, then A and say it, then G. Bag.'

And I make the word. First word.

Bag.

I make the word. I couldn't believe it. I came to make the word. Don't matter what the word is, what it means. Just to make the word. The first word.

That's what caused the trouble. Me and that first word.

I was so excited to be making a word I went everywhere and made the word. I took a stick and rubbed a point on it against a stone and round in back of the quarters I made the word in the dirt.

Wrote *BAG*. Then said it. '*Bag.*'

I rubbed it out with my heel and wrote it in a new place. *BAG*. Wrote it all over. *BAG*. *BAG*. *BAG*. Each time I rubbed it out and moved to a new place and I was just looking at it, last time I wrote it, wondering if I could use other letters to make other words, thinking how to make another word when I hear the bull voice of Waller.

'What are you doing?'

A big hand grabbed the back of my shirtdress and dragged me up off my feet so I be hanging there.

'Tell me what you're doing.' He was ugly. Pale white maggot ugly and I could smell his ugliness on him – white ugly. Stink of bad sweat and whiskey and smoke and fat food. I didn't say nothing.

He shook me like a dog shaking a rat. I felt my eyes go to wobbling and I just about messed. I still didn't say a word.

'What are you scribbling in the dirt?'

I thought, I'll lie. 'Nothing. Something I saw on a old feed sack. I didn't know it was wrong to make it in the dirt.'

'It looks like writing to me.' Holds me up. Closer. Stink of his breath in my face. White stink. Pig stink.

'Don't know nothing about writing.'

He hit me then. Be holding me with both hands, one on each shoulder so I'm facing him, and he quick drops one hand and hits me with his fist alongside the head as I fall.

I saw lights. Exploding colours.

'Don't lie to me. You tell me the truth of it and I'll let you off. Where did you learn to write?'

'Don't know nothing about writing,' I said again. I had dropped all the way down and I was sitting in the dirt looking up at him but it put me in a bad place. Near his feet. Big boots. Black boots but wrong kind of black. Bad black, not good black like John. Mammy. Me. My mind rolled around like a sick dog.

He kicked me in the stomach.

'God damn you – don't you lie to me. I'll tie you to the spring house and get the truth out of you.'

'Don't know nothing about writing....'

He kicked again but he missed. First time I had grabbed my stomach, rolled away, and on the second kick I crawled-ran to get away. Ran to the only place I knew. Ran to the quarters. Ran to mammy.

She be in the corner changing the grease and rag on Alice's back and I ran to her dress and hid my head in the folds.

'What ...?' She held my arm. 'What are you doing?'

'Hiding from him.'

'Who?'

'Waller.'

But Waller, he owned it all. Wasn't no safe place. He owned all the land, owned the quarters. Owned mammy. He came into the quarters then and saw me and took me by the arm. He held me, but he looked at mammy.

'Who is teaching her to read?'

'Sir?' Mammy gave him the big-eyed look. Look like she don't know nothing since she be born.

Waller he stood, looking at her. Breathing. Breath cut in, cut out like a saw cutting wood. I thought of the word, making the word. *Bag*. How making the word can cause all this and I hated myself.

'All right,' Waller said. 'If that's the way you want it.'

And he grabbed. Not me. I made the word but he didn't grab me. He grabbed mammy by the wrist and dragged her out of the quarters and across the dirt to the spring house and shackled her in the chain and bracelets on the wall.

Then he left her there, hanging, and went to the house. I had followed them across to the spring house and when he was gone I went up to mammy.

'He's going to whip you,' I said. I was crying.

She sighed. Soft sound. And she looked up at the sun and the trees by the white house: 'Birds sure do sing nice, don't they? They make the prettiest sound.'

'It's all my doings.' I pulled at the chains but they don't give. 'I be making the word and forgot where I was and he saw me, and now he's going to whip you.'

Her eyes came on me then. I was crying but she wasn't. Her eyes came on me and they were sharp and her mouth was tight. 'He would have whipped me anyway someday. Some other reason would have come along. He loves to use the whip.'

'John.' I thought of him. 'John will stop him.'

She shook her head. 'He can't. No matter what he says, it won't stop Waller from whipping me. Now, you go along and bring me some water when they ain't watching. He won't whip me until close on dark when everybody's back from the field to watch. The sun is hot and I'll be getting a big thirst, don't I get some water.'

I snucked mammy water through the afternoon and she hung there. Way the chains and bracelets were, she couldn't reach down to sit so she had to stand. But standing through the day that way without moving is hard. After it passed some long time her legs didn't do so good and she sagged, and come late in the day she was 'most hanging on the chains. Her arms were up and she was having to hurt. I stood and watched for a spell and cried some but she stopped me.

'You take care of the young ones. Go now. They'll be dirty and stinking, if you don't change the rags on them. You run along. I be fine.'

Took forever, waiting on the day. Mammy hanging that way. I thought once of running to the fields to tell John. Wouldn't do no good. Driver working the fields, he see me coming he just put me to work. They say if you can walk to the fields you can work. So I be working and not here and John couldn't do nothing anyway. They just keep him there no matter what I say.

So nothing.

Walter he keep his white maggot ownself in the white house all the day. Don't come out but once to see me standing by mammy. The sun works across the sky, cooking her. I brought her water again and a piece of cornbread I'd been saving since morning food but she shook her head.

'I'll just throw it up when he comes to whipping me. You go now – get the rags ready for my back and the salt.'

'I can't.'

'Yes. You can. Go do it.'

Finally it came on to be dark and the hands come in from the field. Part of the afternoon I had the young ones to make a trough of cold food so they had enough to eat. They had to walk past the spring house and they saw mammy but there wasn't nothing they could do.

I went up to John and told him what had happened.

'Damn.' He shook his head. 'I should have warned you about making words.'

'I knew. I was just excited. To be making my first word. I got to writing it in the dirt and he caught me. Waller caught me. He's going to whip her. Mammy. Going to whip her into rags.'

John didn't say anything. He looked to where mammy hung on the spring house. His eyes were flat. 'Bastard.'

I was going to say more, say can you stop it, can you say something, but I heard the door on the white house open and Waller came out. He made gas and spit like he'd just ate a big meal and walked across the yard. Stopped.

'All of you get out here and watch.' He bellered like an old bull, then turned. Didn't go to the spring house. Didn't have a whip.

Instead he went to the barn and went inside. Come out in a breath or two and he was carrying a horse harness.

He went to the buggy by the carriage shed and hooked the harness like he had a horse in it, except it was empty.

Then he went back to the spring house. Looked at mammy.

'You going to tell me who's teaching them to read?'

31

Mammy been hanging but she stood now and gave him the big eye again. 'I don't know nothing about reading or writing.'

'God damn you.'

He hit her with his fist. Then he unhooked her from the chains and ripped her clothes from off her body. and dragged her naked to the harness.

'Put it on – I feel like a ride in the buggy.' Mammy put the collar around her neck with the lines going back to the buggy. Stood there. Looking up at the sky. I couldn't keep my eyes down. But the men did, they didn't look at her. Looked at the ground.

Waller climbed into the buggy and sat in the seat. He reached under the footboard and come up with a whip.

'Pull, damn you.'

The whip snaked out from the buggy seat like it was alive and flicked and blood come on mammy's shoulder Big cut. She starred pulling but it wasn't good enough. She strained and heaved and the wagon it moved and Waller kept saying:

'Faster, damn it, faster.'

And the whip come again and again, blood running down her back, the buggy moving across the yard and I hear in back of me:

'She don't know nothing. It was me that taught the girl the letters.'

I turned and John was standing there. He had stepped forward and he pointed to mammy.

'Let her be. She don't know nothing about it. It was all me.'

Waller looked at him the way a cat looks at a mouse caught in a corner. He smiled. Ugly smile.

'Well – I might have guessed.' He stepped down from the buggy and moved to John. 'Why don't you just go over there and put yourself in those irons on the spring house wall?'

I thought John wasn't going to do it. He held for one, two blinks of my eyes. Waller had the whip in his left hand, coiled but ready. His right hand was on the butt of the big pistol in his belt.

Two blinks, then John moved. He walked to the spring house and put the bracelets on. He wasn't wearing a shirt and when he turned his back the sun caught the scars from the old whippings. Rippled and ridged.

There's nowhere for the whip to hit, I thought. Can't hit nothing new. No new meat. Stupid. The way my thinking worked.

But Waller, he wasn't set for whipping.

He made one of the field hands to fetch the stump used for chopping the heads off chickens. Sent another hand to the blacksmith lean-to for a wide chisel and a hammer. Then he turned to us. All standing, watching.

I had moved to mammy but she shook her head. Stood.

'It is wrong to learn to read.' Waller's voice loud, bouncing off the buildings. 'It is against the *law* for you to read. To know any letters. To know any counting is *wrong*. Punishment, according to the *law*, is removal of an extremity.'

We don't know all the words. Never heard 'extremity' before. But we don't need to know.

Waller had two field hands to hold one of John's feet on the block. He put the chisel to the middle toe and swung the hammer.

Thunk.

The toe came off clean, jumped away from the chisel and fell in the dirt. Blood squirting out, all over the block. John he jerked the foot so hard it knocked one of the field hands over. But quiet, not even a grunt out of him. He didn't look down either. Just kept staring off into the fields next to the spring house.

'Other foot.' Waller spit and wiped the chisel off on the stump.

The two field hands grabbed John's left leg. The one next to the wall of the spring house – his name is Robe – he take it slow. Doesn't move fast so you could see it was bothering him and Waller snaps like a breaking stick.

'It can be your toe, too. It doesn't cost more to cut another one off.'

So Robe he puts John's foot up there and Waller puts the chisel on it.

Thunk.

This time was not so clean. The foot jerks back and the toe is caught by some skin the chisel missed.

'Hold it up, damn it.'

They hold the foot to the block. John he still not making any sounds, but his face is stiff. Like it's carved out of rock. And there's sweat pouring off his forehead, his neck, down his chest. He's soaked.

Waller cuts the last bit of skin.

34

'There. That'll teach you to mess with things you shouldn't. Get a rag and some grease on that.'

He walked back to the white house without looking back and as soon as he was away from us we went to helping.

The two hands carried John between them to the quarters and I went to mammy.

'Fetch the salt,' she told me. 'Get it in these cuts and 'fore I pass out for God's sake cover me with something so I ain't naked before the Lord.'

So I did. And she swooned some with the pain and went down. And I frotched her dress and helped to put it on her and then helped her back to the quarters because her legs they didn't work right from hanging and standing all day.

All the time I'm thinking, be a hell, be a good hell with fire and brimstone and devils cutting skin off backs, like mammy says. Be a good goddamn hell with demons, eating at you, pulling your guts out – be the worst hell there is to be. And put Waller in it.

Six

John he down for three nights.

Mammy come up right away, but we grease and wrapped John's feet in rags mammy boiled in the pot for cooking food and he stayed on his back.

For the first night he was quiet and didn't say nothing. Just to lay and look at the ceiling, night and day, except to use a can mammy put there for him to use.

Second night he call me over to where he lay.

'What?' I ask.

'H.'

'What?'

That's the next letter. *H*. It sounds *huhh*, or *hehh*. It's a funny letter because it doesn't make any difference how it stands. Goes up, goes down, doesn't matter. It's the same.'

He makes the letter in the dirt.

H

Mammy she was in the other end and she came walking down to us. The young ones be out playing. Everybody else in the field. I thought she would roar at him, maybe gut him.

But she's smiling.

'Are you addled in the brain?' she asked.

He nodded. On his side, laying like a broke dog. He smiled back. 'I don't get smarter. Just older.'

'You know what he'll do if he catches you teaching letters again? You ain't got so many more toes.'

'Two more nights, I'm gone.'

'On those feet?'

'On these feet.'

'You'll bleed out. I knew you were going, but wait a week.'

'How did you know I was going?'

'You were always going. When you came here they brought you in the collar. You are born to leave.'

John's smile grew wider. 'We should have met some other place.'

'And other time.' Mammy she snorted. 'I make two of you, old enough to be your mother.'

John laughed. Rolling deep sound. 'Maybe so that doesn't matter so much....'

Mammy she went on and he lay back. Looked to me. 'Make the *H*. Make the sound, then the letter. When you get done, fetch me a piece of rawhide from the barn, so big.' He held up his hands. 'I need to make some shoes.'

And in two nights, like he said, he was gone. He made the shoes out of rawhide and put rags around his toes and on the night he was to leave he made me to frotch him lard and pepper.

'For the dogs,' he said. He rubbed the lard thick on the bottom of each shoe and wiped pepper in the lard and stood to leave. 'Throws their smell off to the side.'

Everybody asleep. Even mammy. Except me.

'I'll be back,' he said. 'Got some things to do and I'll be back.'

But I knew he was lying. Just being good, saying the good things to hear. He ain't coming back, I thought, and watched him leave, hobbling on his stiff shoes and sore feet covered with rags.

Man gets out of here, I thought, gets clear again, he won't never come be here again. Never coming back.

Not unless the dogs catched him.

Seven

Wrong again.

Only not right away.

He made it clean away. The next day Waller he took the dogs and two field hands and his horse and set off swearing and stinking. Two days he be gone, and he come back and make a storm around the place so we all know John he made it. He be gone.

Mammy she cried in a happy way and I smiled some for a time and hoped him well, though he left me hanging. I had only the same letters as on both hands. *A, B, C, D, E, F, G, H, I, J.*

I could write them and read them and I took to making words in my head with them. Made *HID*. And *FIB*. And *JAB*. And *HAD*. And *BIG*. Other words. But I didn't dare write them in the dirt. Waller catch me and he'd make a tobacco pouch out of my skin. So I did them in my head, and tried to see the words, see the letters. But summer went, and then we took in crops. Cotton and corn and killing pigs came. Into fall. I still tried to make the letters in my head, and the words.

But my troubles came and though I hid it I knew they'd get to finding out and send me to the breeding shed.

I was in a misery. Mammy she worked to cheer me but it didn't do any good. I was feared and worried day to day that I'd be found out.

Come a night in winter. Leaves gone, pigs all killed and hams hanging in the smokehouse. I sat in the dark, in the corner of the quarters, wishing I could go back a season to where I didn't have the troubles, and I heard a sound next to me in the dark and it was him.

John.

Be right there, next to me.

'Come on,' he said.

'What?'

'Follow me. We got to go so's you can get back before first light.'

'Go where?'

He smiled. Took my hand. Led me to the door. 'School – we got to go to school. Don't you want to learn the rest of the letters?'

'But – '

And we go.

I was never off the place. Been only once to the fields where the corn and cotton grow. John he take me across the fields, out the other end into thick trees, down into some brushy ditches along the river.

Suddenly he stopped.

It be pitch dark. Any light from the stars can't get through the trees and brush and we stand for two, three deep breaths.

Then I smell it. Smoke. Faint smoke and John he leads me down a ditch until we hit a wall of solid brush. The smoke smell is strong now, stink of pitch burning. John he whistle like a catbird and there was a rustle of brush and then a slit of yellow light opened and he pulled me into the brush.

Inside the brush.

There is light, bright yellow from three pitch torches being held by three people. But there's more people there. Same as all on one hand, thumb and the one next to it on the other.

They're all smiling at me. I don't know any of them but they're all smiling. Short boy comes up to me.

'We're from over the hill at the Stankin place. Two from there and the rest from Placers.'

I didn't know nothing about those places but I smiled. back. 'You all know John from before?' He nodded. 'He come at night. Tell us to learn some letters, then tell us to come here. To school.'

I didn't know what a school was, what it was supposed to be. This was slats of brush dragged and pushed over a ditch, thicker and thicker and closed in on the ends.

Be a pit.

Pit school.

John he moved to the end and held one of the torches up. In the other hand he held a book. I'd seen a book. Saw one of the women at the white house looking into one.

'This is a catalog.' John held the book up. 'It is full of things you can send for and own if you have money. They use it all the time. The whites. You read it, and it will tell you things. It has pictures and writing to talk about the pictures. Each of you come up and see it. Be quick now. We only have a couple of hours and I want to give you some letters. Sarny, you know some of them. You help me.'

Everybody look at me.

'Only know this many,' I said, holding up my hands.

'That's a good start. They don't know more than one or two. So you help me until we get to how many you know. Then we can all work together.'

We look at the catalog and I can't believe it. Here in the school, pit school covered over so the light won't show out of the ditch from the torches, we look at the catalog. All the things we don't have. Dresses and shoes with buttons and little gloves and pretty hats and overalls and I started crying. Thinking of all the things, all the pretty things, and then I see it.

Picture of a horse. Got a thing around his head for feeding him, around his head and hanging over his nose.

BAG.

Says it right there. Under the picture. There's other words, but right there it says to me: *BAG.*

'I know this one.' I pointed out the word, the word to John: 'This one right here. It is *bag.* That's a bag on a horse's nose.'

He laughed. Love the laugh. Same deep black laugh. Like night thunder. 'Soon, Sarny, soon you'll be able to read them all. All of you will. Now let's start so you can get back.'

And we do.

I take a stick, rub some dirt clear and draw the lines in the dirt for three of them who watch.

A

Feels good to write again.

Words

Late he come walking.

Late in the night when they in the white house are all asleep and we be asleep and nobody can know nothing, late when the moon is down and the stars are hiding in clouds, late when it isn't the day before and it don't seem like ever the new day will come – that late he come walking.

In the night he come walking. Late in the night and when he walks he leaves the tracks that we find in the soft dirt down by where the drive meets the road, in the soft warm dirt in the sun we see his tracks with the middle toe missing on the left foot and the middle toe missing on the right and we know.

We know.

It be Nightjohn.

Late he come walking and nobody else knows, nobody from the big house or the other big houses know but we do.

We know.

Late he come walking and it be Nightjohn and he bringing us the way to know.

Afterword

This book is dedicated in all honour and admiration to the memory of Sally Hemmings.

While she does not figure directly in the story of *Nightjohn* she caused it to be, and for that reason it is important to understand who she was, how she lived and how she started the work that led to this book.

Sally Hemmings was a slave girl/woman 'owned' by Thomas Jefferson.

I first learned of her some six or seven years ago at the time of this writing (1991) and began trying to find out more about her with the idea of doing a biography.

It was like trying to grab smoke. A bit of information would surface here, another there, some of it apparently valid, much of it not. But always it led – the search led further and further into the world of American slavery, further into the story of *Nightjohn*.

Finally, in sadness, I decided that there was not enough information to write a book on Sally – although there was enough to extrapolate a life, an existence for her, which I will do shortly. But by that time, by the time I realized I could not do a book, she had led me into her life, into her world, into the world of Nightjohn and Sarny.

I wish I could thank her. Sit with her and tell her what she has done for me; how much I have grown from the knowledge she led me to. I wish I could see her. There are no pictures of her – only brief descriptions. She had long brown hair, brown eyes, and was by all accounts stunningly beautiful. There are photographs of her grandchildren and it is possible to see the beauty in them. Among other forms my wife is a portrait artist and she has studied Sally's grandchildren and done a portrait of how Sally may have looked. It is something tangible but, like all knowledge of Sally, it is teasing, haunting. You wonder how she would have smiled, her laugh, the sound of her voice.

What she thought.

She was born and lived in the time and with the man who was the fulcrum of the lever that made the United States of America. Yet she came from a succession of tragedies and violence so raw that even so-called scholars shy away from it.

Sally's grandmother's true or African name is lost, but at some point she was forcibly used by a sea captain named Hemmings. Sally's grandmother gave birth to a daughter from this union and gave her the name of Betty Hemmings. Betty Hemmings was in turn sold to a man named John Wayles, raised, and likewise forcibly used by him. She gave birth to a daughter and gave that daughter the name of Sally.

John Wayles also had a daughter by his white wife and her name was Martha. Probably not too long before Sally's birth, or slightly after, Thomas Jefferson courted Martha Wayles and took her as his wife. Sally Hemmings and Martha Wayles were thus half sisters.

As part of the marriage a dowry came with Martha and in that dowry were many slaves; among them Betty and her year-and-a-half-old daughter Sally. Women then were not allowed to own property and so all the slaves came under the direct ownership of Thomas Jefferson.

Betty was a house slave and Sally was raised in the Jefferson home. At one point during the Revolutionary War Sally, her mother and several other slaves were stolen by British soldiers. The law gave them the right to confiscate rebel property and sell it. But before they could sell Sally and her mother (Sally was then five years old) they escaped and made their way back to the Jefferson plantation.

It is important to note Sally's closeness to the Jefferson family. She was not just raised in the house. She became so close that around the age of nine when Martha fell ill, and subsequently died, it was Sally who became her bedside servant, slept in the same room next to Martha's bed and tended to Martha.

Later – probably at the age of ten – Sally was given the care of the Jefferson white children, and when she was twelve or thirteen she accompanied Jefferson and his children on a trip to Paris. She was to tend the children but there are some intriguing side notes which perhaps indicate other interest.

After meeting her Abigail Adams took a dislike to her, calling her flighty and not dependable. Mrs Adams wrote of this and it is strange that she would take such interest if Sally were only a servant or slave. Jefferson bought Sally expensive clothes, a new dress, had her vaccinated for smallpox (she was the only slave to receive such treatment) about the same time. And there had been some difficulty between Jefferson and a married woman named

Maria Cosgrove. (Apparently her husband came near to challenging Jefferson to a duel.) These are in themselves, perhaps, not important, but put together they show an added interest Jefferson may have had for Sally and that he was apparently open to involvements.

Whatever the reason, somewhere in here – when she was thirteen, fourteen or fifteen – Jefferson began using Sally as her mother had been used and her grandmother had been used.

This relationship continued throughout Jefferson's life. They had many children – probably seven, perhaps more. Four or five boys, two and perhaps more daughters. As time passed and the children grew, some of the boys looked so much like Jefferson that people visiting Monticello would mistake them for him at distance and call them Tom.

Indications are that Sally worked her whole life trying to free the children.

She failed. They remained slaves, property of Thomas Jefferson. Just as she never became free and remained the property of Thomas Jefferson. When he died Jefferson's estate was in virtual bankruptcy and after his death all his property was sold off to pay the debts. There are indications that two of Sally's daughters, who were as lovely as Sally herself – she had educated them, taught them to read, to know, to understand their lives – were auctioned off to a brothel owner in New Orleans to be used for immoral purposes. One of them committed suicide to avoid the horror, the other was dead within a year or so.

The bill of sale for Sally at the same auction read:

One fifty-three-year-old woman.

Worth: fifty dollars.

It is not the intent of this to indict Jefferson. He was by all accounts a man of his time. But to show the system – how warped it was, how incredibly bent and wrong.

An example:

Perhaps the greatest single monument to identify Jefferson and his intellect – aside from the Declaration of Independence – was his home, the estate at Monticello. Much is made of his brilliance at design, at building – what a marvel the house is. They give tours. People come from all over the world to see the house.

Jefferson did not make Monticello. He would no more have picked up a saw or hammer than he would have tried to fly to the moon.

The man who made Monticello – one of them – is on the cover of this book.

He was a master carpenter 'owned' by Thomas Jefferson:

His name was Isaac.

His face is not on Mount Rushmore.

About the author

Gary Paulsen is the distinguished author of numerous books, ranging from Westerns to DIY. He has received great acclaim and many awards for his novels written for young people. Among his best known works are *Hatchet*, its sequel *The Return*, *Tasting the Thunder*, *The Voyage of the Frog* and *The Fourteenth Summer*.

He lives with his family in New Mexico, USA. He has sailed the Pacific and competed in the gruelling 1,049 mile Iditorod dog-sled across Alaska.

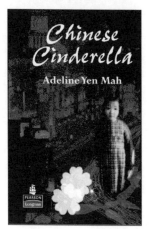